THE CRANE GIRL

based on JAPANESE FOLKTALES

adapted by CURTIS MANLEY

illustrations by LIN WANG

SHEN'S BOOKS, *an imprint of* Lee & Low Books Inc.
New York

For all who helped me find my way to haiku: H.K.D., M.H., the Haiku Society
of America, and especially the members of Haiku Northwest—C.M.

For Megan, Nicholas, Mia, and Helen—L.W.

Special thanks to Michael Dylan Welch
for sharing his knowledge of and passion for haiku and its history.

Text copyright © 2017 by Curtis Manley
Illustrations copyright © 2017 by Lin Wang

All rights reserved. No part of this book may be reproduced, transmitted, or stored
in an information retrieval system in any form or by any means, electronic, mechanical,
photocopying, recording, or otherwise, without written permission from the publisher.
Shen's Books, an imprint of LEE & LOW BOOKS Inc., 95 Madison Avenue, New York, NY 10016
leeandlow.com
Manufactured in China by Imago, January 2017
Printed on paper from responsible sources
Book design by Christy Hale
Book production by The Kids at Our House
The text is set in Zapf Renaissance
The illustrations are rendered in watercolor
10 9 8 7 6 5 4 3 2 1
First Edition

Library of Congress Cataloging-in-Publication Data
Names: Manley, Curtis, author. | Wang, Lin, 1973–, illustrator.
Title: The crane girl: based on Japanese folktales / adapted by Curtis Manley;
illustrations by Lin Wang.
Description: New York: Shen's Books, an imprint of Lee & Low Books Inc.,
[2017] | Summary: A boy helps an injured crane, and the good deed is
rewarded with the arrival of a mysterious guest who weaves beautiful silk
for the family. Includes author's note about Japanese folktales and
poetry, information about red-crowned cranes, and pronunciations.
Identifiers: LCCN 2016005452 | ISBN 9781885008572 (hardcover: alk. paper)
Subjects: | CYAC: Folklore—Japan.
Classification: LCC PZ8.1.M29767 Cr 2016 | DDC 398.2—dc23
LC record available at https://lccn.loc.gov/2016005452

GUIDE TO PRONUNCIATION AND HAIKU

These are the characters' names, how the names are pronounced, and how the haiku showing each character's thoughts is printed.

The boy:
Yasuhiro
yah-soo-hee-roh

The girl:
Hiroko
hee-roh-koh

The boy's father:
Ryota
ree-oh-tah

from the darkness
an animal's sudden cry—
its fear, and mine

Yasuhiro dropped his armload of firewood to follow the sound across the sharp buckwheat stubble of the landlord's field. He almost stepped on the crane, nearly invisible where it lay in the snow. A trap held one foot, but the crane looked unharmed. As Yasuhiro knelt, the bird closed its eyes and shuddered.

Yasuhiro clicked his tongue to calm the bird. "I'm not here to hurt you."

cold hard trap—
he sets me free
with warm hands

When the bird stood up, it was as tall as Yasuhiro. He stroked the soft feathers on its long neck with his fingertips, and the bird gently pressed the red top of its head against Yasuhiro's face.

the crane's head
against my cheek—
how warm it was!

The crane suddenly turned away, began running, and took flight over the wintry hills. Yasuhiro watched until the bird was a pale speck against the dark sky. Then he picked up the firewood his father had sent him for and hurried home.

The next night someone knocked on the door. Yasuhiro opened it and found a girl standing there, pale and shivering, tears frozen on her cheeks.

"Please!" she said, bowing. "I have no home and nothing to eat. May I stay here with you? I will help with chores. I won't be any trouble."

Yasuhiro led her to the warmth of the hearth. "Father will decide whether you can stay."

Yasuhiro's father, Ryota, got up and bowed. "We are not rich like others in town, but you are welcome here as long as you work hard. If you are lazy or steal from me, you cannot stay. Do you agree to that?"

"Yes, sir," the girl said, and bowed again. "Thank you! You may call me Hiroko."

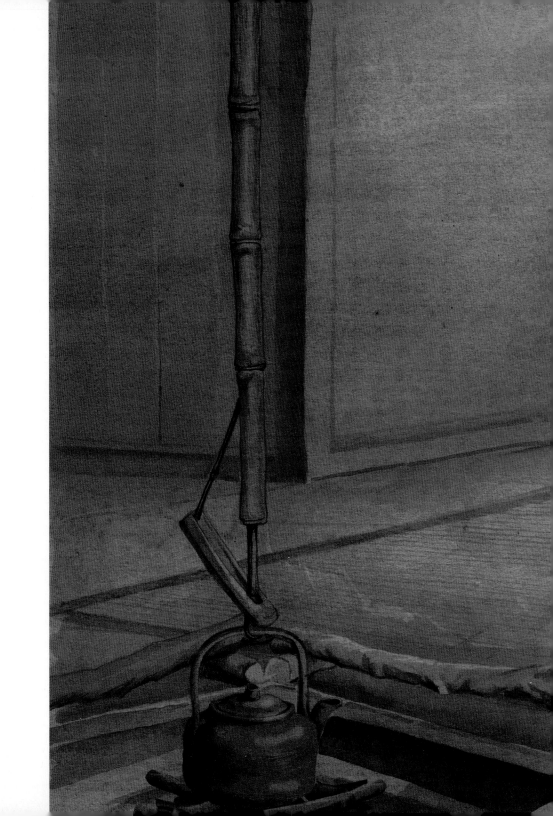

Yasuhiro and Hiroko became friends. They shared their chores and spent their time together.

springtime rain—
I teach her games
everyone else knows

Each morning Ryota walked to town looking for work unloading boats or carrying heavy baskets. He returned in the evening, usually with a fish or noodles. But when he couldn't find work, he came home with only his sadness, crying the name of Yasuhiro's mother.

"Mother died when I was young," Yasuhiro whispered to Hiroko one of those nights. "Father says she wove the finest kimono silk on the whole island. We still have her loom and thread, but Father had to sell all the fabric she made—except my scarf."

"Oh, Yasu, it's so beautiful!" Hiroko said as she stroked the soft fabric.

his mother's love—
threads of all colors
glowing in the weave

The next day Hiroko bowed to Ryota. "If it would please you, Ryota-san, I will weave silk for you. It will bring a good price in the market. I have but one request. Neither you nor Yasuhiro must open the door or look at me while I am weaving. No matter how long I might take. Do you agree to that?"

Yasuhiro and Ryota nodded and said, "Yes."

"Then I will weave for you." She took the bowl of rice and bean sprouts that Yasuhiro offered and closed the door.

my wife's loom—
pounding of my own heart
behind that door

The loom sounded all that night and the next day. Only after dinner did it fall silent. When Hiroko finally opened the door, she was carrying a bolt of cloth as light as a summer breeze.

---

white silk
speckled with black—
tracks of winter birds

A merchant bought the silk for as much gold as Ryota could earn in five months!

heavy sack of coins—
why should I beg
for work?

Now Ryota often slept late. By the time he walked to the village, there was no work left. Instead, he sat with the merchants in the warm sun, eating and drinking all afternoon. The gold was gone in just three months.

So again Hiroko closed the door to weave, taking with her a bowl of tofu and ginger that Yasuhiro had prepared for her.

This time the girl spent two full days with the loom. The fabric was even finer than before!

weightless silk—
her trembling hands
and tired eyes

A merchant paid so much that Ryota stopped even trying to look for work. He went to town only to sit by the docks with the merchants and boast of the fine silk he would weave for them.

cup by cup—
his father swallows
all the money

In a few months, all the gold was spent again. "More cloth!" demanded Ryota.

Hiroko looked down at the floor. "I am still too weak, sir. Next month I will weave more."

"You will do it now!" insisted Ryota, and before Yasuhiro could stop him, Ryota pushed the girl into the room and slid the door shut. Yasuhiro looked at the door and remembered his promise to Hiroko never to open it.

---

knock of her loom—
I put down the chopsticks
and stare at my rice

A day passed, and then another. The loom's rhythm seemed slower with each passing hour. Ryota paced back and forth.

three days!
how those merchants
must laugh at me

Finally the loom fell quiet. "Are you done with the cloth?" Ryota asked, and slid the door open. He cried out and fell back onto the floor.

Yasuhiro rushed toward his father but stopped and stared. Through the open door he saw a long, thin neck and feathers flecked with blood. And then a great wing slammed the door shut.

Ryota ran past Yasuhiro and stumbled outside into the darkness.

---

even the moon gone—
all my good luck
lost again

When Hiroko finally came out, her face was pale and her eyes were red from crying. "Yasu, here is the silk for your father. Once he sells it, he need not bear any burdens for many months."

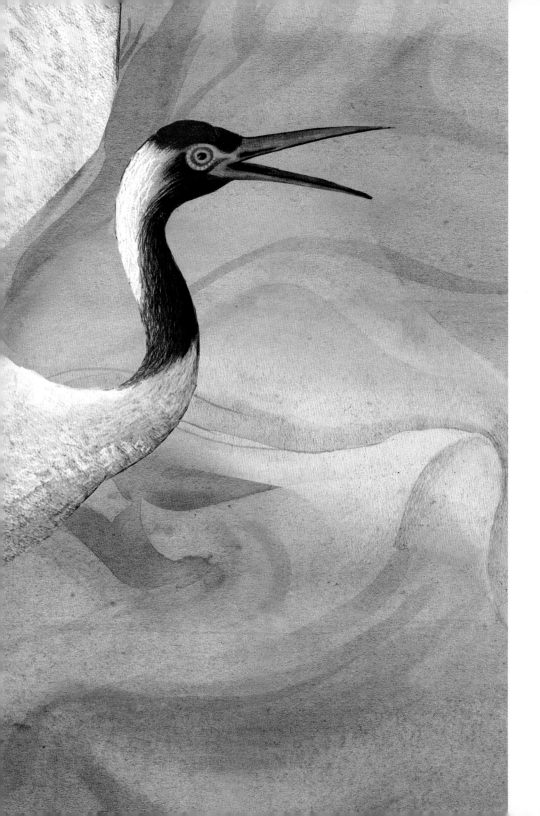

"I'm sorry about Father," Yasuhiro said, gazing down at the fabric. Hiroko pressed her head against him.

the last time
I will touch his cheek—
cold tears

Yasuhiro thought of what he'd seen through the open door, and touched Hiroko's neck. "Why did you pluck your own feathers for the cloth?"

"You saved my life when I was caught in the trap," said the girl. "You were so gentle and kind I wanted to be with you."

Hiroko's feathers—
her love for me
threaded through the silk

Hiroko pulled away from him. "But I can stay here no longer." She hurried outside, and within three steps changed back into a crane and flew away.

everything lost—
how could he ever love
a crane?

Yasuhiro ran and ran, calling after her and sobbing. When she was just a dark speck in the dawn sky, he could run no more.

He must have fallen asleep, for suddenly Hiroko was bending over him. "Yasu! Go home! You will freeze here in the snow."

"I won't go back," said Yasuhiro. "Take me with you."

Hiroko shook her head. "Our life is too different. It is a hard life. You wouldn't like it."

"I will like it—because I'll be with *you*."

"Then follow me." She began running. "And flap your wings hard!"

"But I don't have . . ." But he did. He did have wings.

matching
her wingbeats—
my heart soars

———

Together they flew low over the hills and along the river to the marshes at the edge of the sea. Her people clacked their beaks in welcome and danced for them.

Yasuhiro and Hiroko stayed together all the rest of their long lives and raised many crane children, one by one by one.

———

spring sun—
our chick's feathers
wet from the egg
  how lucky we all are
  to be cranes

AUTHOR'S NOTES

CRANE FOLKTALES

Folktales were told and retold by wandering Japanese storytellers for hundreds of years. Storytellers often changed a tale for the specific audience they were entertaining. Even well-known tales have many versions that differ in details but share the same plot.

This adaptation of the crane story is based on several beloved folktales from Japan, where a multitude of retellings of them exist. In the West, only two versions are known well. In *The Crane Wife* (*Tsuru Nyobo*), a young man rescues a crane and then gives shelter to a mysterious young woman. They fall in love and get married, but when she begins weaving wonderful cloth, his greed and curiosity drive her away. In the version known as *The Grateful Crane* (*Tsuru no Ongaeshi*, literally "the crane's return of a favor"), an old, childless couple gives shelter to a young woman, but again the crane leaves when her identity is discovered.

In other versions written down by Japanese folktale collectors in the early twentieth century, different animals—such as a wild duck, a wild goose, and even a white rat—take the place of the crane. These and many other collected folktales are described and discussed in *The Yanagita Kunio Guide to the Japanese Folk Tale*, edited and translated by Fanny Hagin Mayer (Bloomington, IN: Indiana University Press, 1986).

An important theme in all these versions is the Japanese concept of *on*—an obligation that must be repaid. The rescued animal feels compelled to return the favor to the human who saved her life. When the human breaks the one agreement they have—not to look while she is weaving—the obligation ends; the animal gives up her human form and leaves her rescuer forever.

I have loved these tales for many years but wanted to create a version in which it is a young boy who saves the crane and befriends and loves the crane girl, but who is not greedy or at fault when the girl's true identity is revealed. Although the crane must leave, she is able to keep her connection with the boy who rescued her. The transformation of the boy into a crane is my own addition; humans are changed into animals in some Japanese folktales, but it is less common than animals assuming human form. Even with these changes, all the traditional elements of the tale remain intact.

JAPANESE POETIC FORMS

Haiku (pronounced "hi-koo"; the plural is also *haiku*) is the best-known form of Japanese poetry. In Japan, it is written in one line, vertically down the page. Elsewhere in the world, it is usually written in three short horizontal lines. Although many people are taught that a haiku must have a pattern of 5-7-5 syllables, this is not strictly true. In Japan, counting 5-7-5 refers to Japanese language sound symbols, which are different—and shorter—than English syllables.

Most contemporary poets who write literary haiku in English do not try to force their haiku to fit the 5-7-5 rule. Instead, they try to keep their haiku no longer than about seventeen syllables (most often around ten to fourteen syllables) and pay more attention to including a reference to the season, using images based on one or more of the five senses, and presenting the poem in two parts (one of the parts being spread over two lines). The separate images or ideas of each of the two parts can interact in surprising ways—and can make a haiku very powerful even though it is such a short poem.

Other poetic forms are based on or related to haiku. Many poems that look like haiku are actually senryu (pronounced something like "send you"). Whereas haiku usually concern the seasons and have a serious tone, senryu (singular and plural are the same) tend to be about human foibles and often poke fun. *Haibun* (pronounced "hi-boon") is a Japanese term used for prose

writing that contains one or more haiku or senryu—like this story. *Haiga* (pronounced "hi-guh") combines a painting with a haiku in calligraphy. The type of poem at the end of the story, written by two people in collaboration, is known as a *tan-renga* (pronounced "tan-ren-guh").

Haiku is very popular in Japan, and nearly a thousand haiku clubs exist where members can improve and share their poetry. There are similar groups in the United States and other western countries, such as the Haiku Society of America, Haiku Canada, the British Haiku Society, and smaller regional and local organizations.

JAPANESE NAMES

Many Japanese names have special meanings. Yasuhiro can mean "honest" or "peaceful," Hiroko can mean "generous child," and Ryota can mean "stout" or "strong."

THE RED-CROWNED CRANE

The red-crowned crane (*Grus japonensis*) is the second-rarest species of crane. Fewer than three thousand of them remain in the wild. Many red-crowned cranes spend their summers in northeastern China and Siberia (eastern Russia) and then migrate to warmer areas for winter. One group of the cranes, however, lives year-round on the Japanese island of Hokkaido. Laws now protect those birds and the land they live on, and food is put out for them in winter fields and marshes.

For hundreds of years, Japanese people have considered the crane a symbol of happiness and long life. Songs, poems, and stories about the crane are popular, and wedding kimonos are often sewn from fabric woven with crane designs.